Samuel French Acting Edition

Careless Love

by John Olive

SAMUEL FRENCH

SAMUELFRENCH.COM   SAMUELFRENCH.CO.UK

FOR PRODUCTION ENQUIRIES

UNITED STATES AND CANADA
Info@SamuelFrench.com
1-866-598-8449

UNITED KINGDOM AND EUROPE
Plays@SamuelFrench.co.uk
020-7255-4302

Each title is subject to availability from Samuel French, depending
upon country of performance. Please be aware that *CARELESS LOVE*
may not be licensed by Samuel French in your territory. Professional
and amateur producers should contact the nearest Samuel French
office or licensing partner to verify availability.

MUSIC USE NOTE

Licensees are solely responsible for obtaining formal written permission from copyright owners to use copyrighted music in the performance of this play and are strongly cautioned to do so. If no such permission is obtained by the licensee, then the licensee must use only original music that the licensee owns and controls. Licensees are solely responsible and liable for all music clearances and shall indemnify the copyright owners of the play(s) and their licensing agent, Samuel French, against any costs, expenses, losses and liabilities arising from the use of music by licensees. Please contact the appropriate music licensing authority in your territory for the rights to any incidental music.

IMPORTANT BILLING AND CREDIT REQUIREMENTS

If you have obtained performance rights to this title, please refer to your licensing agreement for important billing and credit requirements.

CARELESS LOVE premiered at The New American Theater, in Rockford, Illinois, J. R. Sullivan, Artistic Director, on April 26, 1984. Sets and lights were by Michael S. Philippi and costumes were by Jon R. Accardo. The production was stage managed by Tim Olds Clark and it was directed by J. R. Sullivan.

JACK. . . . . Tim Halligan
MARTHA. . . . . Susan Bolin

CARELESS LOVE has also been produced by: Wisdom Bridge Theatre, Actors Theatre of St. Paul, The Empty Space Theatre, The Hartman Theatre, The Oregon Stage Company, the Society Hill Playhouse, and others.

Special thanks to Jim Sullivan and the New American Theater.

CAST

JACK, early 30's
MARTHA, early 20's

PLACE

Chicago

TIME

During the spring and summer

SETTING

The play takes place in Jack's apartment and on a bare stage area which will represent, variously, a restaurant, a phone booth, a street, etc. The apartment is a typically messy actor's flat, with exits, right, to the kitchen and the apartment hallway and one exit, left, to the bedroom. The bare stage areas can be in front of the apartment or off to the side, depending on the playing space. It is also possible for the apartment set to be moved on and off, during those scenes (mostly at the beginning and very end of the play) which are not set in the apartment.

Careless Love

ACT ONE

AT RISE: JACK alone. HE's holding a rolled-up play-script and waiting, glancing around nervously, looking quite out-of-place.

JACK. I spent my first five years in Chicago pretending I lived in a Jack Kerouac novel. It was easy, really. I'm an actor. I'm Irish. (*beat*) You know, my draughty three room flat, Wrigley Field a picturesque three blocks away, the el screeching romantically through the Sheridan Avenue curve all night. Do the show, close the bar, read till dawn, breakfast in the bleachers. Series of bizarre relationships with theatrical women. Or theatrical relationships with bizarre women, whichever. And the work was good, too. Or so I thought, at the time. Chicago theater was growing and even, I thought, getting better. Plenty of opportunity for a guy like me, with a good voice and some catchy mannerisms, you know, the actor's bag of tricks, to get some work. And starve, romantically. La vie boheme. It was great. Five years. The happiest, shallowest years of my life. (*to someone offstage.*) Hm? No, thanks. Hm? I'm waiting for someone. Hm? Martha. Say, listen, does she know I'm here? I told whatshername, the maitre d'. The hostess, right. Maybe she forgot to tell Martha I'm here. Oh, no, I'll just wait here. I'm fine here. Thanks. (*Beat: JACK paces a bit, opens his script, then closes it. Then HE speaks quickly, impulsively.*) Well, see, the way it works is, we spend all our lives stepping over these bloody festering corpses, strewn all over the floor, everywhere. And we refuse to talk about them. We're polite, and politic and optimistic. We kiss and smile and shake hands, and we can barely breathe because of the stench. "Hi, nice to see you, we could all die at any moment, maybe we're at ground zero right now." "Oh, not bad, how's yourself?" (*beat*) Some spring very soon, the snow's gonna melt, but the grass won't grow, ain't nothing gonna grow. We'll all be living on plastic flowers and Twinkies. (*beat*) There's an ancient Chinese curse: may you live in interesting times.

(*MARTHA Enters. SHE's wearing a waiter's apron.*)

MARTHA. Oh.
JACK. It's me.
MARTHA. Hi, Jack.
JACK. Hi, Marty. How are you?
MARTHA. Fine. What do you want?
JACK. You get off pretty soon?
MARTHA. I still got some customers.
JACK. Wanna have a late lunch?
MARTHA. Well, I usually eat here. They give us a pretty good discount.
JACK. The lunch you have with me'll be free. I'll pay for it. Marty.
MARTHA. What?
JACK. I've been thinking about you a lot.
MARTHA. That's nice.
JACK. Look, I feel like a jerk dropping in like this, but you don't have a phone.
MARTHA. You know how expensive phones are these days? It's really crazy.
JACK. But phones come before food, don't you know that?

MARTHA. Tried to call you.

JACK. Really?

MARTHA. All's I get's your machine.

JACK. So leave a message.

MARTHA. I don't have a phone you can call me back on.

JACK. I'd like to talk to you.

MARTHA. What about?

JACK. What about?

MARTHA. What do you want to talk to me about? (*to someone offstage*) Yes? (*to JACK*) Just a sec. (*Exits*)

JACK. Her name is Martha. Known to her intimates, an exclusive club, apparently, of which I seem to find myself a charter member, as Marty. We were in *A Midsummer Night's Dream* together. She played one of the fairies. She's a dancer. I thought she was the answer to all my sexual prayers. God, she was beautiful. (*beat*) She thought my Bottom was brilliant. I agreed. My first Shakespeare. I was making twenty-five dollars a week over scale. I was a star. It was her first professional job, she thought I was a star. The critics nailed us to the wall, but I didn't mind, I was having a great time. (*smiles*) I knocked up a fairy. (*MARTHA enters.*) You still pregnant?

MARTHA. Yes.

JACK. When do you get off?

MARTHA. I don't really know.

JACK. But can you try to guess?

MARTHA. I have a party of twelve still. A birthday party. Thirty minutes.

JACK. Meet me across the street. Please.

MARTHA. The Foxy Lady?

JACK. No, Marty. O'Rourke's. On the corner. Please, I want to talk to you.

MARTHA. What about?

(*A moment: JACK looks at her closely, then reaches out to touch her face. MARTHA steps away, avoiding him, looking away.*)

JACK. I've missed you.
MARTHA. Oh yeah? (*tense beat*) Okay.
JACK. What?
MARTHA. O'Rourke's. Okay.
JACK. Half an hour.
MARTHA. I gotta go.
JACK. See you there. (*MARTHA exits.*) Spring in the city. The sky is yellow and the grass is blue. The Cubs won the opener. And I love you.

(*JACK sits at a table. HE opens his script, studying it, sipping at a glass of Guinness stout, glancing up from time to time. A long moment. MARTHA enters. SHE hesitates, looking at JACK, then comes to his table.*)

MARTHA. Hi!
JACK. (*slightly startled*) Oh, hi. I thought you weren't coming.
MARTHA. Birthday party started drinking champagne, and, well, you know. . . .
JACK. Champagne drinkers.
MARTHA. Yeah.
JACK. Animals. (*short beat*) Well, I'm glad you came. Sit down.
MARTHA. Well, okay. (*SHE sits, and takes the script, opens it.*) This the new play?
JACK. Yeah.

MARTHA. "Little Criminals." (*pages through the script*) Which are you?

JACK. Andrew.

MARTHA. (*reads*) "Gone to seed attorney. Less intelligent than he thinks. Drinks." (*starts paging through the script*)

JACK. (*watches her for a short moment*) The first act is very weak. I'm not in it. (*pauses*) Page forty eight. (*MARTHA reads.*) I could recite it.

MARTHA. No.

JACK. Want a beer? (*reads from a card on the table*) Molson, Moosehead, Dab, Harp, Guiness, Bass, Dos Equis, Carta Blanca and please stop me, Marty, before I go entirely insane.

MARTHA. No, thanks, Jack, I don't want any beer.

JACK. Okay. (*reads again*) Inglenook, Blue Nun, Gallo. Marty.

MARTHA. Nothing.

JACK. Perrier? Virgin Mary? Coke?

MARTHA. Nothing.

(*Beat. MARTHA continues to read. JACK gently takes the script from her hands, and sets it aside. MARTHA looks away; suddenly, SHE looks lonely, upset.*)

JACK. Are you okay, Marty?

MARTHA. I'm fine.

JACK. Are you . . . sick at all? In the mornings or something?

MARTHA. Little bit. Mainly, I'm tired.

JACK. Do you feel like there's really something . . . I don't know, weird, going on with your body? Something basic?

MARTHA. I'm pregnant.

JACK. Oh, okay, right. (*takes a pull of his beer*) How 'bout those Cubbies? (*beat*) Marty. I'm sorry about the other day, if I behaved badly.

MARTHA. When?

JACK. The other day. At the theater. You remember the little scene at the theater?

MARTHA. Scene?

JACK. Well, whatever you want to call it, it was a scene. The folks at rehearsal were all moved.

MARTHA. You're a very good actor.

JACK. (*stares at her, shocked, then laughs*) Look, this is hard. I mean, normally this is something that happens between people who know each other pretty well.

MARTHA. I'm sorry this is hard for you.

JACK. Do you really hate me?

MARTHA. Not at all. You were a very good lover.

JACK. (*after a slight pause*) Okay. Do you need some money?

MARTHA. Money?

JACK. For . . . an abortion? All I wanna do is whatever's the right thing. (*quick beat*) You know Stuart, the guy I was talking to at rehearsal when you came in? After you . . . left, he said, "Well, Jack, are you going to do the right thing by that girl?" And I said, "Marry her?" He looks at me, big dramatic pause, and says, "Pay for her abortion." (*pause*) Well, anyway, do you need money? I . . . got my checkbook.

MARTHA. (*not looking at JACK*) I made an appointment today, at Planned Parenthood.

JACK. Oh? They have abortions there? It's not just . . . pills and rubbers?

MARTHA. They have referrals to abortionists. They

send you someplace else, to get the abortion. All they do is, they advise you.

JACK. (*after a slight pause*) When's the —?

MARTHA. (*overlapping JACK*) And if you need — (*stops*)

JACK. Go ahead.

MARTHA. And if you need money or something, they can advise you about that.

JACK. Well, I can pay for . . . I can help you pay for the —

MARTHA. It happens really fast. They stretch your vagina open, with a . . . thing. Then there's this long needle, they showed me one, they use it to inject Novacaine into your cervix. That part hurts. Then they stretch your cervix open, and then they . . . suck the baby out, with a vacuum. Then they scrape the rest of it out, then they suck it all clean, and that's it. Easy. (*pauses*) Then you have a lot of emotional problems afterwards, lots of . . . anxiety, because of all the . . . Well, I guess you lose a lot of hormones.

JACK. Do you want me to go down there with you?

(*MARTHA laughs, abruptly and rather shrilly.*)

JACK. What's so funny?

MARTHA. That's not what you're supposed to say!

JACK. Tell me what I'm supposed to say! Tell me what to do! This is hard! You feel like a total stranger to me, and you wouldn't believe the load of Irish Catholic guilt I'm carrying about this.

MARTHA. You get guilty, I get pregnant.

JACK. (*Now JACK bursts out laughing. Then an abrupt beat: HE covers his face with his hands, weeping.*

Finally:) Well, fuck you. You have as much responsibility in this as I do.

MARTHA. I don't expect anything from you. If all you want is for this to be over, then okay, it's over. I won't bother you any more. The guilt is your problem, I'm sure you can take care of that alone, I'm sure you've had lots of practice.

JACK. (*staring at her*) Jesus Christ.

MARTHA. I only told you because I thought you had a right to know.

JACK. As the father.

MARTHA. Yes.

JACK. You know, Marty, I was given to understand that your sex life was pretty varied and active, as they say.

MARTHA. Who gave you to understand that?

JACK. Persons who would, at this point, I'm sure, prefer to remain anonymous.

MARTHA. Well, they were wrong! You're the first person I've made love with since I left school.

JACK. Since . . . ?

MARTHA. Almost three years.

JACK. That's great! Luck 'o the Irish, eh? Your first time out in three years and you get zapped!

MARTHA. I'm not Irish.

JACK. But I am! (*stands abruptly*) Well, you're not getting shit from me, the price of an abortion, and that's it. (*brandishes his script*) I got work to do! Gotta go fake and bullshit my way through another piece of shit play, the ole crazed Celtic charm strikes again. I should thank you, I'll be able to use all this in Act Three! (*starts to exit, then turns; in a fake-theatrical voice*) Good-bye, darling! (*Exits. MARTHA alone. JACK enters his apartment, slamming the door. MARTHA stands and moves downstage. She's isolated in a spot. JACK pushes the start button on his answering machine. SFX: The SHARP TONE of the machine.*)

MARTHA. (*looking straight ahead*) Jack, this is Martha. I'm using the machine. I hope you're not listening to this at home, 'cause I really don't wanna talk to you. I tried to go to that awful clinic again today, it was the second time I went, and I can't . . . do it. Some women can, I guess, but not me. Did you know that a twelve hour old fetus has a heart? You have to suck and rip 'em away from the uterus, you have to use stainless steel needles, have you ever seen those things? It has a heart! (*beat*) Well, anyway, I'm telling you now, I'm not gonna do it. I'm not sure what I am gonna do, but I don't want anybody . . . telling me what to do. I'm gonna have a baby. It's exciting. I'm — (*SFX: the sharp BEEP of the machine, cutting her off. Pause. SFX: another BEEP*) I was going to say I was sorry. Well, I'm not. Your play opens on May fourteenth. Work well. And don't worry, I'm okay, I'm very good at being okay. Break a leg. Me too, eh? (*pauses briefly*) Bye. (*Beat. Then the LIGHTS on the restaurant foyer area intensify. JACK and MARTHA step into the area.*) You gonna yell?

JACK. I'm not gonna yell.

MARTHA. I'm not supposed to have visitors here. Don't disturb the—

JACK. (*yells*) I'm not gonna disturb the customers!

MARTHA. (*laughs, a nervous release*) Jack. . . .

JACK. Oh, so you think this is funny? (*MARTHA tries —without success—to stifle her laughter.*) Stop laughing at me! Marty! Marty!

MARTHA. (*upset now*) Jack. (*beat*) Just . . . take it easy. (*Another beat: THEY look around self-consciously.*)

JACK. (*takes a deep breath*) So whaddaya gonna do?

MARTHA. What?

JACK. What are you going to—

MARTHA. I'm gonna have a—

JACK. Baby! You can't do that, god damn it, it's my baby, too, you can't just . . . have it. In Chicago, the city I work in, how'm I supposed to live with that? I'm an actor, I can't be a father! (*stops*) I shouldn't be here. I don't wanna get you fired. I'm an asshole. (*quick beat*) You don't have the faintest idea what you're doing. Having a kid. Christ. How old are you?

MARTHA. Twenty-two.

JACK. (*slight pause*) Oh, God. Do you know how to do this? You eating all the right foods? You supposed to be on your feet all day, waiting tables. Stupidity is bad for babies.

MARTHA. I'm not crazy.

JACK. But you're out of your mind! God.

MARTHA. (*smiles, after a beat*) It was that first night.

JACK. What?

MARTHA. It was incredible that night. It was more than just horniness, it was instinct to reproduce.

JACK. (*looks at her*) Really? Can they pinpoint it like that, or are you just being . . . poetic? (*laughs*) God.

MARTHA. Nobody ever filled the way you did. (*hands on her belly*) I can still feel it. (*looks offstage*) I gotta get back to my section. You gonna be okay?

JACK. Yeah, well, I'm working. You know.

MARTHA. Break a leg in the play. (*Exits*)

JACK. (*after a short pause*) You, too.

(*Moment: JACK alone. Then a slow fade to BLACKOUT SFX, in the darkness: the El, RUMBLING AND SCREECHING as it goes by Jack's apartment. This sound will recur periodically throughout this scene.*

*LIGHTS fade up: Jack's apartment, late at night; it's
dark. Noises off: FOOTSTEPS in the hall, a KEY in
the lock, etc. JACK Enters. HE turns on a LIGHT,
then goes into the kitchen, returning with a bottle of
imported beer. HE checks his answering machine.)*

JACK. Alright! *(Turns the machine on, and ups the
volume. HE paces the apartment, unbuttoning his shirt,
taking long swigs of beer, in something of a hurry. SFX,
the first message: a DIAL TONE. JACK tosses his shirt
on the sofa, checks his armpits, and decides on a new
undershirt. HE takes off his undershirt and Exits into the
bedroom. SFX, the second message: a DIAL TONE.
From offstage:)* Damn it. *(Re-enters, with a fresh undershirt; HE starts buttoning a new shirt, pacing and swigging beer. SFX, the third message: DIAL TONE. JACK
glares at the machine. Then HE remembers something.)*
Oh. *(Takes several newspaper clippings—reviews—
from the pocket of his discarded shirt, gets a few pushpins
and pins them to the apartment door. SFX, the fourth
message: a DIAL TONE.)* Damn it! *(goes to the machine, presses the record button and dictates a new message, in a silky, actorly voice)* This is Jack's answering
machine. Jack's not here right now, but I know he'll be
very curious as to who's been calling. So, look. Please.
Do the right thing, okay? Leave your name and a message. Hey, thanks.

*(HE tucks in his shirt, standing by the door, reading the
reviews. HE finishes his beer, grabs a jacket, turns
out the LIGHTS. HE opens the apartment door.
MARTHA is standing in the hall.)*

MARTHA. *(very startled)* Aaaggghhh!!!

JACK. (*very startled*) Aaaggghhh!!! (*JACK slams the door shut.*) What the hell! (*Opens the door. MARTHA's still there, clutching her beating heart.*) Marty!

MARTHA. Jeez, Jack, you scared me.

JACK. What the fuck are you doing!?!

MARTHA. (*nervous*) Well, I . . . was gonna knock, but I . . . Well, I heard you talking to someone, I didn't wanna . . . disturb you.

JACK. Talking to — Oh.

MARTHA. I better go. (*SHE leans down and picks up a large, overstuffed backpack. SHE shoulders it and moves into the hallway, out of sight.*)

JACK. (*steps into the hallway*) Hey! What are you doing, camping out? What's the matter with you?

MARTHA. (*offstage, not visible*) Nothing, nothing. I'm —

JACK. (*off*) Landlord told me, he said any more women camping out in the hallway and I was out, superstar or no superstar.

MARTHA. (*off*) Jack, sh. (*JACK steps into the hallway, out of sight by now.*)

JACK. (*offstage*) You still pregnant?

MARTHA. (*off*) Yes.

JACK. (*off*) Really? Any religious visions? Throw up all the time? Getting really connected to Mama Earth?

MARTHA. (*off*) You alone?

JACK. (*off*) Yeah. (*beat*) You okay?

MARTHA. (*off*) Yeah. (*beat*) Can I come in? (*Moment. Then JACK enters, carrying the large backpack; HE dumps it heavily on the floor. MARTHA follows him in.*)

JACK. Whaddaya got in here?

MARTHA. Everything I own.

JACK. So you just packed up everything you owned

and came over to see me at . . . (*looks at his watch*) Ten fifty P.M.? Flattering.

MARTHA. Who were you talking to?

JACK. My public.

MARTHA. Running lines? (*Laughs, covering her mouth with her hands, a nervous giggle. JACK stares at her, deadpan. Pause. MARTHA stops laughing.*) I saw the play.

JACK. Little Criminals? When, tonight? You saw the play tonight?

MARTHA. Yeah, I got a hot tix.

JACK. Why didn't you come backstage?

MARTHA. I don't like to do that. It's too scary backstage, right after a play.

JACK. How'd you get over here?

MARTHA. On the el.

JACK. What a coincidence, I took the el home, too.

MARTHA. I know. (*JACK is staring at her.*) Can I have a glass of milk?

(*Short moment, then JACK exits, into the kitchen. Noises off: FRIDGE opened, closed, MILK POURED. JACK comes back with a glass of milk; HE gives it to MARTHA.*)

JACK. Lemme know if it's too racy.

MARTHA. Racy?

JACK. Well, it says one week beyond the date stamped on the carton, but —

MARTHA. (*sips it*) It's fine. (*short pause*) Thanks.

JACK. (*after a pause*) Oh! I got it! You hated the play. You thought I was dreadful, you were embarrassed for me, and that's why you didn't come backstage.

MARTHA. You were wonderful, Jack.

JACK. Oh, you don't have to say that.

MARTHA. You really were. You and Amanda.

JACK. You liked Amanda?

MARTHA. There's nothing better than good acting, it's like food. The constant sense of self-transformation, always searching, always trying to become something . . . beyond what we are, it's exciting. (*JACK is staring at her.*) What's wrong?

JACK. Don't stop! Oh, God, I crave this, it's like gentle rain from heaven. Food?

MARTHA. Huh?

JACK. I gave a food-like performance? (*Beat; MARTHA looks away.*) Look. I'm supposed to go to this cast party tonight, and —(*MARTHA stands up, abruptly, spilling her milk a bit.*) Amanda's having us all for—

MARTHA. I can go. I'll go now. You have to go to your cast party, and—

JACK. Marty.

MARTHA. I'm sorry, I shouldn't've bothered you. Can I leave the—? No, I better—

JACK. Marty! What are you so afraid of?

MARTHA. I don't know. Nothing. I'm fine. (*beat*) It's nice to see you. You look pretty good to me. You gonna be able to be a star with that beerbelly? (*beat*) Aw, jeez.

JACK. I'll have you know, young lady, this cost me more than two thousand dollars.

MARTHA. (*hands on belly*) This one was free.

JACK. Growing a belly?

MARTHA. Pretty soon. (*THEY look at each other for a long, charged moment.*)

JACK. Okay. When the going gets weird, the weird have a beer.

(*Exits. MARTHA looks around the place. JACK appears in the kitchen door, with a bottle of beer. SFX: the EL passing by.*)

MARTHA. You can hear the el.

JACK. Yes. You hear it in the morning and you know: the world's survived into another day. It's very reassuring. I have to pay extra for it.

MARTHA. You were so good tonight. I was so proud of you.

JACK. Notice the reviews? That I am brilliant in the play is a unanimously agreed upon fact. (*reads*) "Incandescent." "Frightening comic intensity, combined with a masterful sense of timing." (*As HE reads, his shoulders start to sag; HE turns.*) Impressive, eh? Gives you gooseflesh, right? I fooled 'em. Pulled the wool over their eyes yet again. They all think I'm terrific. They think I'm an "important" talent! (*sits*) And now guess what. I'm up for a piece a shit TV pilot, about a bunch a guys in a lunch truck, going around to factories and warehouses, meeting all kinds a wacky people. If I get it, I'll have to sign a five year contract, in case it's a big hit. (*pauses*) Going camping?

MARTHA. Sort of.

JACK. Sort of. Ooh, enigmatic and cryptic. I'd like to be able to say I enjoy camping, but it would be a lie. I'm into room service. It's very bizarre to see you. I really haven't been thinking about you and . . . the little critter. Too busy being incandescent. You know.

MARTHA. Can you kiss me?

JACK. Kiss you?

MARTHA. Yeah, I think I want you to kiss me.

JACK. (*Pause. JACK takes a swig of beer, then goes to*

MARTHA, hesitating.) Kiss. (*A kiss, perfunctory at first, then growing more intense. JACK breaks it off, moves away.*) Well, look at us, kissing and hugging and smiling, you'd think the world wasn't even on the brink of nuclear disaster. (*sits*) So. (*short pause*) Well, let's see, you thought the play was swell. Great.
MARTHA. Remember Sylvia?
JACK. No.
MARTHA. She did the choreography for *Midsummer.*
JACK. Oh, right. I asked her out.
MARTHA. She's a lesbian.
JACK. (*slight pause*) I knew that.
MARTHA. She's teaching at that Black River Summer Institute in Wisconsin. They have work-study scholarships and she recommended me, and I got one! She gets two recommendations. I got it! I get room and board, free classes and five dollars an hour for working in the food service. The food's really good there. (*gets a brochure out of a pocket on her pack, gives it to JACK*) Here.
JACK. (*glances at the brochure*) You're gonna study dance all summer?
MARTHA. Yeah. Oh, I'm like really excited.
JACK. Do pregnant women dance?
MARTHA. You gonna be stupid now?
JACK. It's a serious question. Do pregnant women dance? I mean, what is art?
MARTHA. Everybody dances.
JACK. Oh! Yes! Of course! Life as solo dance recital. Is it good for the baby? There's a real sense now, whereby your life is no longer your own. This is the eighties, and you don't support a baby on five dollars an hour, part time.

(*Long pause. MARTHA is staring at the floor, very em-*

barrassed. SHE looks up at JACK, then looks away, very up set and nervous. JACK watches her calmly.)

MARTHA. (*finally*) Jack.
JACK. Yes, Martha?
MARTHA. I . . . Well, I gotta ask you for a . . . like a really big favor.
JACK. Okay.
MARTHA. Can I stay with you for a few days, just till Thursday, when I go up to the Institute with Sylvia? I asked Sylvia, but she's . . . Well, she has a guest. I was gonna ask Maria, my boss at work, but then she fired me.
JACK. You lost your job!?
MARTHA. They were so weird about me bein' pregnant. "Don't say anything to the customers," and I woulda had to quit when I started to show anyway. Then what happened, my dad called me there. He knows I won't ever talk to him, so he tells Maria it's a "family emergency." I was yellin' and swearin' at him, right at work. Then Maria fires me. (*pauses*) My mom died in January.
JACK. Oh. (*quick beat*) January! That's when we were working on *Midsummer*! I had no idea . . .
MARTHA. I was with her when she died. (*hands on her stomach*) Maybe this is her, eh?
JACK. Marty, Jesus.
MARTHA. My dad with with his new girlfriend mosta the time, and now they're married. And he thinks I'm crazy! (*beat*) My roommates got somebody else. I didn't wanna pay a whole month's rent, just for four days. I don't have hardly any money, is the thing. (*beat*) Worrying about money's an incredible narcotic. I'm not gonna give in to it. (*MARTHA smiles at JACK.*) You really were incandescent. Different from Bottom. Bottom was

. . . big, and explosive, all your energy went up, into the clouds. But tonight, you were so alive, you made everybody else look like store dummies.

JACK. (*slight pause*) Aw, shucks.

MARTHA. That's why she's here, you know, 'cause you were so funny as Bottom. I had a dream about you.

JACK. Oh?

MARTHA. I dreamt you were pregnant.

JACK. Ah.

MARTHA. Yeah, and I was running my hand over your belly, and I could feel the baby's head, arms, feet. I could feel it where your penis was supposed to be. It was a boy.

JACK. Kind of an interesting dream there.

MARTHA. It means I'm going to have a girl. (*laughs lightly*) We were in bed together. No. You were in bed. And I came in and you said, "I'm going to show you something." And you lifted the sheet, and I could . . . see it. (*Beat. MARTHA smiles, then coughs, looks away, coughs again.*) Oh, no. (*SHE starts to cry, softly, still smiling.*) Oh dear.

JACK. Hey.

MARTHA. It's okay, don't worry, I'm fine. I am. This is just something I . . . do. (*coughs again, then sobs*) Oh! (*smiles at Jack*) This is all pretty lonely.

JACK. Well, yeah, I can imagine.

MARTHA. I don't know too many people in Chicago. And you know how tough the first trimester is.

JACK. Oh, yeah, right.

MARTHA. I feel wonderful. I do. I've never been so involved with my body before, not even when I was studying dance. My blood feels so rich. And my heartbeat. Sometimes, like right now, I can hear my heart, it goes, "Pregnant. Pregnant. Pregnant." Sometimes I can't hear anything else. (*laughs*) It's my secret. Tonight, on the el, everybody was staring at me. I've got a secret! They're all afraid a me. Jack!

JACK. Huh?

MARTHA. (*slight pause*) Don't you be afraid a me.

JACK. I'm . . . not.

MARTHA. I'm very powerful. Sometimes, I just know things. Like I know you're gonna be a star.

JACK. (*laughs uncomfortably*) Marty, I don't think so. Lately, I've really been hating my work.

MARTHA. I didn't say you were gonna like it. (*pauses*) You better get going. And thanks for letting me stay here. I really . . . like you. It's nice to see you for real, not just . . .

JACK. On stage.

MARTHA. In a dream.

JACK. Well, Marty, it's . . . nice to . . . see you. Too.

(*Pause. Then JACK goes to her, sits, puts his arm around her shoulders, holding her. MARTHA relaxes, leaning into jack, her eyes closed. It soon becomes obvious that MARTHA's asleep—and heavy. JACK slowly lowers her onto the sofa. HE Exits into the bedroom SFX: the EL, rumbling past. JACK returns, with a blanket and a pillow; HE slips the pillow under MARTHA's head and covers her with the blankets. HE slips her shoes off, then turns off the apartment LIGHTS. A tableau: JACK stands for a moment, looking down at MARTHA, watching her sleep. LIGHTS FADE slowly to BLACKOUT. After a moment, LIGHTS fade up: JACK's apartment, in the afternoon. MARTHA is futzing with the answering machine. Her pack lies next to her, on the floor.)*

MARTHA. *(pushes a button)* Jack? Testing. *(Pushes the replay button: nothing. SHE tries another button.)* Jack? Hi! *(Pushes replay: nothing again. Tries two buttons at the same time.)* Jack? *(pushes the replay)*

MARTHA'S VOICE. *(on the machine)* Jack?

MARTHA. Okay. *(clears her throat, gets ready to record, finally pushes the two buttons)* Okay. Jack, I gotta go up to—Oh. This is Martha. Your pregnant pal. I'm leaving you a message with the dictation button. I'm going up to the Institute two days early, 'cause Sylvia's going up with a bunch a people in a van. I've never been in a van before. I'm sorry I can't go to the ballgame with you, I was really looking forward to it. I've never been to a baseball game before. *(SFX, from outside: a HONK-ING HORN.)* I'm coming!! Jeez. So, anyway—*(The door opens, and JACK Enters, carrying a bag of A&P groceries. MARTHA is very startled.)* Aaaggghhh! *(SHE releases the buttons.)* You always scare me when you come in. How come you're here?

JACK. I . . . live here. *(refers to her pack)* What's . . . ?

MARTHA. I gotta go. Sylvia's giving me a ride up to the Institute, she's going a couple days early, she decided. They're waiting outside.

JACK. Oh.

MARTHA. Yeah, so I . . . gotta go. Oh! *(unzips the side pocket of her pack, takes out a small newspaper)* Lookit I found on the el. *(gives it to JACK)* It's one of those suburban newspapers. There's a review in it. Page eight.

JACK. Am I prominently mentioned?

MARTHA. Oh, sure.

JACK. Look, Marty, I don't know if you should go up there. I mean, in your . . . condition, and everything, there's probably bears up there. Ticks.

MARTHA. I'll be okay.

JACK. I keep forgetting to remember that, don't I?

MARTHA. Yeah. (*pause*)

JACK. You need some money?

MARTHA. Oh, no.

JACK. Don't you have to help pay for gas?

MARTHA. Well, I don't know. I don't get a check until a week from Friday.

JACK. (*takes out his wallet*) I got . . . fifty two dollars.

MARTHA. I don't want that much.

JACK. Well, take—

MARTHA. Just gimme one of the twenties.

JACK. Take both twenties.

MARTHA. Just one. I don't need—

JACK. Take 'em both.

MARTHA. Just give me—

JACK. Take both the twenties! (*stuffs the bills into MARTHA's pockets*) Damn, this is nuts, I don't believe this, I think I may be losing my mind here.

MARTHA. Thanks.

JACK. When you coming back?

MARTHA. The conference is over July fifteenth.

JACK. Call me when you get up there, okay?

MARTHA. I don't like long distance phone calls. They . . . hurt.

JACK. Please call me. Collect.

MARTHA. No. (*beat*) You okay?

JACK. Me? I'm fine. Well, you know, I'm . . . working.

MARTHA. Well, I wanted to say . . .

JACK. Don't mention it. (*SFX: HONKING HORN outside.*)

MARTHA. I'm coming! (*to Jack*) I gotta go. (*shoulders her heavy pack, goes to the door, turns, smiles*) Bye.

JACK. Take care of yourselves.

(*MARTHA Exits. A moment, then JACK goes to his answering machine, pushes the playback button.*)

MARTHA'S VOICE. Okay. Jack, I gotta go up to — Oh. This is Martha, your pregnant pal. I'm leaving you a message with the dictation button. I'm going up to the Institute two days early, 'cause Sylvia's going up with a bunch a people in a van. (*JACK goes to a window, watching Martha getting into the waiting van.*) I've never been in a van before. I'm sorry I can't go to the ballgame with you, I was really looking forward to it. (*LIGHTS begin a slow fade.*) I've never been to a baseball game before. I'm coming!! Jeez. So, anyway — Aaaggghhh!

(*BLACKOUT. LIGHTS fade up: JACK's apartment, late at night. MARTHA is vaguely visible, on the sofa, asleep. JACK Enters, carrying a brown paper bag. HE quickly puts the bag down, and hurries into the bedroom. Noises off: JACK PISSING. After a moment, JACK re-enters, goes to his answering machine, peers at it.*)

JACK. If you don't turn the machine on, you don't get any messages. (*HE lovingly removes a bottle of German beer from the bag, then takes the bag into the kitchen. Noises off: FRIDGE opened, BEER POPPED open, etc.*

JACK comes back in, swigging his beer; HE goes to the sofa and sits on MARTHA.)

MARTHA. AAAGGGHHH!!!

JACK. Jesus Christ! Jesus Christ! (*HE leaps off the sofa.*) Jesus Christ! (*Holds his palpitating heart; beer is dripping over his hand onto the floor.*)

MARTHA. (*sits up*) Jack?

JACK. Marty. Marty?

MARTHA. Yes.

JACK. I'm gonna die. This is it. My life is passing before me. It's very boring. Marty. God almighty

MARTHA. I fell asleep. I didn't mean to fall asleep.

JACK. You're back. From wherever you were, for three weeks longer than you were supposed to be.

MARTHA. I tried to call you from the bus station, but your machine's not working, so I took the el up. I still had a key. Are you alone?

JACK. Yes.

MARTHA. Oh, good. (*pauses*) Hi.

JACK. Hi. (*Turns on a LAMP, and the room gets brighter. MARTHA looks very soiled and roadworn—like her pack.*) You look like shit. Where the hell've you been? I thought you were coming back in July. (*looks at her closely*) You okay? Oh, sorry, I forgot, you're always okay. (*realizes he's covered with spilt beer*) Excuse me. (*Exits into the kitchen. From offstage:*) I got your card. Thanks. (*re-enters, with a fresh beer and a towel*)

MARTHA. What card?

JACK. The one you wrote me, letting me know where you were, just in case I mighta been worried about you.

MARTHA. Your beerbelly's bigger.

JACK. It is not. (*beat*) The play closed tonight.

MARTHA. Really.

JACK. You missed the thrilling finale. Thirty-seven people in the house. You're looking at an unemployed actor. But my incandescent performance lives on, in theatrical legend. The cast said its tearful farewells. Amanda stuck her tongue in my ear. Where the hell've you been.

MARTHA. I went on a canoe trip.

JACK. A what?

MARTHA. Canoe trip.

JACK. You went on a canoe trip? Where?

MARTHA. Minnesota. Part of the time we were in Canada.

JACK. With who?

MARTHA. Sylvia. Bunch a people from the conference.

JACK. (*suddenly bursts into laughter*) A canoe trip! In the great north woods! Woman in the Wilderness. With child. Making her Primeval Pilgrimage. Catch any fish? See any bears?

MARTHA. I saw two bears and a moose.

JACK. I saw a corpse on an el platform. Luckily, it was an A stop and I was on a B train.

MARTHA. (*speaking slowly, very tired*) I rode a bus all the way from Two Harbors, Minnesota. First to Minneapolis, then on to Chicago. Fourteen hours.

JACK. I can smell you from here.

MARTHA. I haven't had a real bath in about three weeks.

JACK. (*slight pause*) You stink.

MARTHA. I tried to go swimming, but I got a cramp and I almost drowned.

JACK. Well, Pocahontas, welcome back to ground zero. You want a glass of milk?

MARTHA. Oh, yes! I was gonna go ahead and have some, but . . . Well, I wasn't sure I should.
JACK. You couldn't help yourself to a glass of milk?

(*MARTHA shrugs, looks at JACK, then looks away, embarrassed. JACK goes into the kitchen, returning with a glass of milk. MARTHA drains half of it, thirstily, then wipes her mouth with the back of her hand.*)

MARTHA. Thanks.

(*A long pause. MARTHA sips her milk, not looking at JACK; as JACK speaks, we begin to see that she's very upset, and having trouble staying calm.*)

JACK. (*after a moment, swigging his beer*) So how you been, Jack? Well, to tell you the truth, Martha, not so good. Lonely. Miserable. The el's been keeping me awake. And the play, God, I was completely dishonest, faked my way through the whole thing. Another perfectly decent play destroyed by Jack the Hack. I despised the cast. I'm almost, *almost* glad to be unemployed. This is the first time I've been out of work in more than a year. I get very snarly. That's a warning. (*beat*) Something's changing, eh? Don't you feel it? (*long swig of beer*) Well, I've made a decision. When they pull the big trigger, I wanna be at ground zero. I wouldn't wanna be in the great north woods. (*beat*) I wanna be on stage. (*beat*) I keep wondering what it'll be like, being suddenly transformed into a gas. Will I last long? Will I be able to communicate with anyone? Like the schmuck in the front row. "What a drag, eh? The end of human civiliza-

tion." As we float up into eternity. "Good riddance."
(*MARTHA slams the milk glass down on the table, then
covers her face with her hands. Short beat.*) What's—?
    MARTHA. (*shouts*) OH GOD!!! (*pause*)
    JACK. Well, okay. Enough about me. How are you,
Miz Marty?
    MARTHA. I don't have any clothes.
    JACK. Me either.
    MARTHA. Jack, I don't know what I'm gonna do. I
don't have a place to live. I don't have a doctor. I don't
even know where I am.
    JACK. You seem to be . . . here.
    MARTHA. I rode that bus for fourteen hours. I couldn't
move. I couldn't sleep. I thought I was gonna lose my
mind. I couldn't breathe. I have a baby in here! A baby!
(*beat*) And look at me. My body's just goin' *nuts* on me.
And those awful people I was with, and it rained every
day, this cold, slimy rain, every day.
    JACK. I see. A nameless, all-pervasive, dripping sense
of dread.
    MARTHA. Yes.
    JACK. Are you sure you're not Irish?
    MARTHA. (*laughs, in spite of herself*) It's not funny!
    JACK. Yes, it is! Everything's funny!
    MARTHA. It's not . . . funny. (*And SHE laughs, gig-
gles; it grows and builds, oddly and intensely. JACK
watches her.*) Maybe I am crazy, huh? Jack, I need help, I
don't know what I'm gonna do. I was thinking, maybe I
should go to a . . . home, but—
    JACK. Nuns, yes, they'd love to get their hands on you.
    MARTHA. All I could think about, up there, was here.
This place. This couch. The el. Milk.
    JACK. (*slight pause*) Me?

MARTHA. Well, yeah. Can I stay here tonight? (*A moment: JACK sits next to MARTHA.*)

JACK. How much money you got?

MARTHA. Don't yell.

JACK. Have I ever yelled at you?

MARTHA. I got forty-three dollars in my pack.

JACK. (*takes a long swig of beer*) Well. That's . . . great.

MARTHA. But my old landlord owes me a hundred and fifty for my damage deposit. Plus interest. He better give it to me, or I'll be pissed.

JACK. Do you type?

MARTHA. Yeah.

JACK. Temps! I used to hang out with this person, Betsy, she was heavily into temp agencies. It's like being an actor, you gotta keep buggin' 'em, and pretty soon they get you some work, just to keep you out of their hair. We'll rehearse your winning smile, get you a brass wedding ring.

MARTHA. A ring?

JACK. Yeah, well, most employers prefer pregnant women to be married, it's sort of an American folk custom. You might have to lie.

MARTHA. I don't lie.

JACK. You might have to. Then we'll get you a nice Nancy Reagan frock and you —

MARTHA. I don't lie.

JACK. Why not, you somebody special? You'd have to lie to get on welfare! (*quick beat*) Look, you made the decision to carry this kid, so now you gotta do it. Lie when you gotta lie. Cheat, borrow, snatch purses from old ladies. That thing in your belly is real! (*beat*) Call your dad.

MARTHA. No.

JACK. This is what dads are for!

MARTHA. Nooooooo!!! (*Laughs again, and again it builds intensely. SHE stands, moves across the room, forcing herself to calm down, hands covering her face. We—along with JACK—see her clearly for the first time; SHE's wearing soiled cast-off clothing, and there is an unmistakable curve at her stomach. JACK stares at her. MARTHA looks at him, calmer now.*)

JACK. You really are starting to show.

MARTHA. Yeah. Everything. My breasts, my belly, my ass, my thighs, my face, I'm starting to feel like a walking freak show.

JACK. Can I . . . feel? (*goes to her, gently puts his hands on her stomach*) It's hard. Resilient.

MARTHA. This little curve, sometimes the whole world bends around it.

JACK. Goes all the way down to your . . .

MARTHA. My womb.

JACK. We'll have to get you one of those tee shirts that say "BABY," with the arrow pointing down to— (*MARTHA suddenly embraces him, impulsively, passionately.*)

MARTHA. Oh, God, Jack!! (*HE's surprised, but returns the embrace.*) I'm so glad to see you.

JACK. (*a bit embarrassed*) Yeah, well, I can understand that.

(*MARTHA laughs, and kisses him; the kiss grows rather quickly sexual. A long moment, then MARTHA breaks it.*)

MARTHA. Oh.

JACK. Yeah.

MARTHA. I haven't made love since we . . . got pregnant.
JACK. Me either.
MARTHA. Maybe I better take a bath.
JACK. (*after a beat*) No.

(*Another kiss. LIGHTS fade slowly to BLACKOUT.*)

END OF ACT ONE

ACT TWO

Scene: *LIGHTS fade up: JACK's apartment, in the af-
    ternoon. Empty stage.*
At Rise: *JACK enters, through the front door, holding a
    rolled-up script.*

Jack. Hey, fatso! You around? Say, Miz Marty, I
bring news from the front. You here? Come hear the
thrilling tale of the Irish wonder's exploding skyrocket to
immortality! (*MARTHA Enters.*) Fatso! (*HE looks at
her: SHE's wearing a pair of baggy brown work pants,
recently taken in and shortened.*)
   Martha. Hi.
   Jack. Good God, those are mine. You take 'em in
yourself?
   Martha. Yeah. They feel good. I love old cotton.
   Jack. Madame Onassis got nothin' on you.
   Martha. What?
   Jack. And you can let 'em out, as you . . . blow up.
   Martha. Thanks.
   Jack. As you grow and expand, I should say.
   Martha. Thanks for the pants.
   Jack. You can get into my pants any time you want.
   Martha. What skyrocket:
   Jack. Oh, yes! The ongoing saga of the beerbellied
Irish superstar. I had lunch with Anita today.
   Martha. Anita?
   Jack. My agent. You met her at *Midsummer*, re-
member? And I got an industrial!
   Martha. Oh.
   Jack. Isn't that great? Here's the script, I read it on the
el. It's . . . Well, it's stirring. I play a young life insur-
ance salesman, just hired. And I'm nervous, in a new

36

world, confused, frightened. In pain. But I've got to get going with this thing, got to save the world from a lack of life insurance. And I can do it, I know I can. But, my God, the extent of life insurance ignorance in this world, it's sickening. So I have to learn the ropes. I learn psychology. I learn to dress for success. I rehearse with practice customers. Did you know that when the customer says no, that's the start of the sale? Fascinating stuff. At the end, I walk out into the world, ready, prepared, confident.

MARTHA. I went to the doctor today.

JACK. (*looks at her for a quick beat*) Wait a minute, the good part. I get three days work at three hundred seventy five dollars a day. (*Hesitates, then exits abruptly into the kitchen. From offstage:*) You okay?

MARTHA. Yes.

JACK. (*off*) Good! (*Enters, holding a bottle of beer; HE takes a swig.*) And the kid?

MARTHA. Well, the baby's alive.

JACK. Alive!? Jesus, did you think he was dead?

MARTHA. She. I listened to her heartbeat.

JACK. Yeah? What's it sound like?

MARTHA. Like a heartbeat. Fast and soft, like the wings of a dove.

JACK. (*laughs*) Like the—(*stops himself*)

MARTHA. You have to use a special stethoscope.

JACK. Musta been a thrill. Motherhood. The tom-toms of our ancestors. The mystery of life. What's the matter?

MARTHA. (*not looking at Jack*) I didn't have enough money to pay. I didn't think it would be so. . . . Well, tests and everything.

JACK. (*hesitates*) Well, okay, I confess. (*takes out his wallet*) I got some money. Anita had a check for me, God love her. Residuals. I love residuals. They're rerunning that pizza thing I did. In Dayton, Ohio. (*removes some currency, counts it*) Impressive, eh? "Gosh, honey, look at that wad! Think how much he must have in the bank!" How much do you need?

MARTHA. The doctor said I didn't have to pay.

JACK. What kinda doctor would say that?

MARTHA. My doctor.

JACK. This charity, or does he just like your face?

MARTHA. She.

JACK. She!

MARTHA. She said I could apply for Medical Assistance.

JACK. What's that?

MARTHA. Welfare.

JACK. Fuck Welfare! Here. How much was the bill? Take—(*MARTHA exits, into the bedroom.*) Wonderful. Shit. (*beat*) Hey, guess what. Anita says I'm up for a movie. A TV movie, about a guy who goes to nursing school, mainly to get laid, but then he really gets into helping sick people. Then he falls in love with a doctor. A woman doctor. (*MARTHA re-enters, holding some printed material.*) I figure maybe T minus one month on the bursting skyrocket to fortune and fame.

MARTHA. (*gives the brochures to JACK*) She gave me this stuff.

JACK. (*glances through it, tosses it aside*) Condescending bullshit. And now I suppose we're gonna have legal aid shysters and social workers pounding on the door. Nuns. How can you let those people treat you like that? Fuck that. (*Beat. JACK moves away; MARTHA doesn't look at him. Then JACK holds out money.*) Here.

MARTHA. It's not enough.

JACK. How much do you need!?

MARTHA. (*after a beat*) Well, they told me how much it costs to have a baby.

JACK. Oh?

MARTHA. In Chicago, with hospital, doctors' fees, medications, and . . . postnatal stuff, well, the average cost is three thousand two hundred dollars.

JACK. Many happy returns. (*beat*) Well, maybe you shouldn't have her in the hospital.

MARTHA. Well, where'm I gonna have her?

JACK. Hospitals are so . . . sterile.

MARTHA. That's how come they're so expensive.

JACK. But there's alternatives to that—

MARTHA. My doctor says no.

JACK. Of course she's gonna say no, she works for the bloody hospital. Look, I just thought you might be into . . . natural baby-having, since you're so . . . I don't know what I'm talking about.

MARTHA. (*after a pause*) I have to be in the hospital, because there's sort of a . . . Well, there's a slight chance there's a . . .

JACK. What?

MARTHA. It's no big deal.

JACK. What is it?!

MARTHA. Well, depending on what happens during . . . labor, it turns out I might be sort of . . . small.

JACK. Down there?

MARTHA. My pelvis. Here and back here. She said I might be a little tight, she wasn't sure.

JACK. Let's get sure.

MARTHA. The only way to do that is to take an x-ray, and you can't do that.

JACK. (*slight pause*) Why not?

MARTHA. The radiation can damage the baby.

JACK. Oh. So she just measured you, with her hand?

MARTHA. Maybe. She put some other stuff up there, too.

JACK. Makes a guy sorta wanna cross his legs.

MARTHA. So there's a slight chance they'll have to do a C-section.

JACK. Slice you open and take her out the easy way.

MARTHA. This is pretty scary.

JACK. It'll be alright.

MARTHA. That's what she says.

JACK. That's what all doctors say, that's why they're so expensive. (*beat*) Well, you should be scared, it's a scary thing. Reproducing. Bringing forth new life, mewling and puking into the cold world, it's gonna be a major pain in the ass. And expensive, as it turns out, a cool grand a day. They must wait on you hand and foot. Very labor intensive. Ha ha. Hey, maybe they'll let us wash dishes at the hospital, did you think to ask about that? (*stands, starts moving about, energy increasing*) Coupla unemployed actors, reproducing. Coupla creative, talented, extremely well-adjusted guys, getting our genes into the human pool. There's an enormous world-wide shortage of actors. (*MARTHA has taken out another piece of literature.*) What's that?

MARTHA. (*gives it to him*) It's a directory of—

JACK. Adoption agencies! (*JACK is upset; HE paces the room briefly, then turns to look at Martha. A moment between them, then JACK looks away, and sits. HE puts the directory down. Finally:*) That what you're gonna do?

MARTHA. It's . . . just something they gave me. I don't know, they just . . . gave it to me.

JACK. So what do they do, they take her right after

she's born? They give you a chance to say hello? Or good-bye?

MARTHA. I don't know. They . . .

JACK. Hm?

MARTHA. They pay for everything.

JACK. Well, it makes sense, I suppose. I mean, there's the issue of the next twenty years of your life. The problem with babies is they grow up to be kids. And how do you feed 'em, you put a bowl of lettuce on the floor, or what? They need braces, they get in trouble with the nuns, plus weight allowances on the skyrocket to fame and fortune are very restrictive. Baby makes one too many. Think of your career. (*MARTHA has her arms folded in her lap, and is rocking back and forth, looking straight down. JACK watches her.*) Am I upsetting you?

MARTHA. I don't know if I can do this.

JACK. Do what?

MARTHA. This.

JACK. Of course, you can do it, you think you have a choice?

MARTHA. You're not helping.

JACK. Tell me what to do! You won't take my money, you won't let me go to the doctor with you, you —

MARTHA. You can listen to me!

JACK. I do listen to you!

MARTHA. You do not!

JACK. I do too!

MARTHA. You don't!

JACK. (*slight pause*) Oh yeah?!?

MARTHA. All's you do is, you make jokes.

JACK. Well, it's funny. If you can't make things funny, then things are nothing more than . . . what they are, which is not very funny. (*MARTHA's crying.*) Aw, damn it. Stop crying. Look, I may be an asshole but I'm harmless. Sort of . . . charming, don't you find me sorta goofy and disarming? (*pauses*) You wouldn't do that, if you knew how it made you look. (*kisses her on the forehead*) It's nice to have someone here after an exciting day of superstardom. (*kisses her again*) It'll be okay. It'll be hard, but some day she'll thank you for it.

MARTHA. You make me feel like I'm your little girl.

JACK. My little girl!? You're not my — (*stops himself, staying calm*) I don't want a little girl hanging around here. Little girls don't get pregnant.

MARTHA. You treat me like —

JACK. I do not! You're buggin' me now. 'Scuse me. (*exits into the kitchen, then abruptly returns*) No wonder they treat you like shit, you dress like you just stepped out of a production of *Annie* at a home for unwed mothers. (*Exits. Noises off: FRIDGE door opened, beer opened, etc. MARTHA suddenly puts her hands on her stomach, and giggles softly.*)

MARTHA. Oh.

(*JACK re-enters, with a beer.*)

JACK. (*looks at her*) What's so humorous?

MARTHA. Tickles.

JACK. What tickles? (*figures it out*) Oh! Oh. She . . . ? Really?

MARTHA. I can tell when she's asleep, and when she's awake, when she's happy, and when she's pissed off.

JACK. (*fake-cool*) Hey, no kidding.

MARTHA. Wanna feel? C'mere, I'll introduce you. C'mon. Whatsamatter, you scared?

JACK. Scared? Me? Hey, I don't know the meaning a the word. (*Hesitates briefly, then goes to MARTHA, and puts his hand on her stomach. MARTHA lifts her shirt, puts his hand on her bare skin.*) I don't feel anything.

MARTHA. There.

JACK. (*snatches his hand away*) That was you.

MARTHA. No.

(*JACK tentatively puts his hand back on her belly.*)

JACK. (*slight pause*) Well, c'mon, make the little bastard do it again.

JACK AND MARTHA. There.

JACK. (*again snatches his hand away*) Okay! Yes, indeed. Gosh and golly. That's pretty . . . real. (*JACK swigs his beer.*) You hungry at all?

MARTHA. No, but the doctor says I should eat more. I'm too skinny.

JACK. I got eggs, cheese, scallions, I could make a kickass omelette. How's that sound? (*Exits into the kitchen. NOISES off.*) Anita's going on vacation next week, and I'm starting to develop serious separation anxiety about it. What if the Big Call comes in?

MARTHA. Jack?

JACK. Yeah, Mama?

MARTHA. Maybe I should move out.

JACK. (*still offstage*) Move out? (*re-enters, stands in the doorway, holding a wire whisk*) You're kidding.

MARTHA. I don't wanna get in your way.

JACK. You seriously wanna leave this lap of luxury? Wrigley Field as convenient as it is, the comforting sounds of the el all night? My magnetic personality? (*pauses*) Well, you do what you need to do. But keep in mind, I'm happy to have you . . . Both.

(*A beat, then JACK exits. MARTHA alone. LIGHTS

fade slowly to BLACKOUT. SFX: a Cubs game, heard on the RADIO. LIGHTS fade up: Jack's apartment, in the afternoon. JACK paces the place impatiently, listening to the radio, wearing a Cubs cap, looking out the window. NOISES off: a key in the lock. JACK goes quickly to the door. MARTHA enters.)

JACK. Where the hell've you been? It's already the second inning, and if the bleachers're sold out and we have to sit in the grandstand, I'm going to be very crabby. Let's go.

MARTHA. Jack, I—

JACK. C'mon.

MARTHA. I gotta change, I have to—

JACK. You look great, you don't have to change. Well, here, you might need a hat. (*grabs a baseball cap, puts it on her head*) Today's tote bag day. Well, c'mon, the Cubs're only behind one run. (*HE looks at her, for the first time: SHE's very excited, grinning.*) Come on.

MARTHA. I can't go.

JACK. You can't go!? What do you mean you can't go! I been waiting for you!

MARTHA. You coulda gone by yourself.

JACK. I don't wanna go by myself, I always go by myself, I wanna go with you. I been fantasizing about taking you to the Cubbies for weeks. It's like Christmas in there, you won't believe it. (*pauses*) Why can't you go?

MARTHA. I got a job. And I gotta—

JACK. A job? You got a job?

MARTHA. Yeah.

JACK. A job-job? How'd you manage to pull that off?

MARTHA. I read an ad in the Reader, and I applied. And they hired me. I'm a receptionist.

JACK. Oh.

MARTHA. It's an insurance company. It's not far, just over on Halsted. Their regular receptionist is on maternity leave, so they hired me.

JACK. They like 'em pregnant.

MARTHA. They like me! And I didn't have to lie, Jack, they know I'm not married, and they don't care. They know all about you.

JACK. And they hired you anyway?

MARTHA. One of the bosses there knows who you are, he saw you in Mother Courage.

JACK. Did he think I was good?

MARTHA. I can pay rent now!

JACK. You don't have to pay rent.

MARTHA. I want to.

JACK. I'm the one who pays the rent around here.

MARTHA. But you're unemployed, so I —

JACK. Thanks for reminding me, jeez, I'd forgotten all about that! I knew there was something bothering me, and you managed to put your finger right on it! Thanks. (*short beat*) This is wonderful news. You got a job. Eight hours a day.

MARTHA. And half days on Saturdays.

JACK. That's great. Now I get to watch soaps, drink beer all day and be depressed, all by myself.

MARTHA. (*after a pause*) So go to the ballgame.

JACK. I don't wanna go to the ballgame without you! (*SFX: the crowd at Wrigley Field ROARS, building and growing; a home run for the Cubbies. JACK looks out the window, listening.*) Life is passing me by. (*takes his cap off, tosses it onto the sofa*)

MARTHA. You're not going?

JACK. Naw. I gotta go down and groove with the brothers at the unemployment office, you know.

MARTHA. Well, I'm excited!
JACK. Me, too.

(*MARTHA exits into the bedroom.*)

JACK. Me, too.

(*Exits, through the door. LIGHTS fade to BLACKOUT. SFX: the RUMBLING AND SCREECHING of the el. LIGHTS fade slowly up: JACK's apartment, late at night. JACK's asleep on the sofa, a fan blowing directly on him, wearing only shorts, clearly a hot and humid night. NOISES off: someone fumbling with keys, finally getting the key in the lock; the lock turns. The door flies open, banging against the wall. JACK stirs. It's MARTHA: SHE stands in the door- way looking flushed, sweaty, slightly crazed. SHE paces behind the sofa. JACK is stirring, becoming aware of her presence.*)

MARTHA. (*Looks at him. In a loud voice.*) Nice weather —
JACK. (*sits up, startled*) Huh!?
MARTHA. —we're having, huh!
JACK. Oh. Well, if it isn't Martha, the wacky pregnant girl. (*rubs his eyes*)
MARTHA. (*still pacing*) The air's green. You can't see farther than two blocks. I oughta have my head exam- ined. Bringing a new person into this stinky world. Screws loose all over the place. Huh? Right, Mr. Wit?
JACK. (*looks at her*) You okay? What time is it? (*Looks at his wrist — no watch. Exits into the bedroom; from offstage:*) It's almost midnight.

(*MARTHA sits, taking cushions from the couch and putting them under her stomach, as support, lying on her side.*)

MARTHA. I think my breasts grew about two more inches tonight. (*laughs again*) Dancing's like being a fish in the air. Everything disappears, 'cept the dance, and you're flying along the bottom of an ocean of air. (*sits up abruptly, picks up an empty ice cube tray*) You didn't fill up the ice cube tray again.

JACK. (*after a slight pause*) Mea culpa.

MARTHA. What?

JACK. That's Irish for I feel real guilty. Marty.

MARTHA. (*drops the tray on the floor*) Selfish. (*lies back*) Aaaggghhh. . . . (*sits up again, turns the fan up to high volume, focuses it directly on herself*)

JACK. Marty. (*Turns the fan down, moves it. MARTHA grabs it roughly, turns it back to full blast, laughing.*) God damn it! (*Stands, moves away. Beat.*) Well, I didn't get that play.

MARTHA. What?

JACK. I didn't get the play.

MARTHA. What play?

JACK. *Tartuffe*! I was called back for it, I told you about it, at some length.

MARTHA. Oh, yeah.

JACK. I didn't get it.

MARTHA. Too bad.

JACK. Stuart got it.

MARTHA. Oh, he's very good.

JACK. He's wonderful. I wish him the best. I'm proud to be the schmuck he aced out for Orgon.

MARTHA. You didn't think you were gonna get that part, anyway.

JACK. But that doesn't mean I didn't want it! I never think I'm going to get any of the parts I audition for. I'm a shit actor, nothing but gimmicks and some sort of crazed Irish charm. So nothing till November at least. It's been years since I went this long between jobs. I think maybe I've lost it. I've been telling myself I'm a hack, and now it turns out to be true. Poor, self-deluded Jack. I should give it up. Marry you and sell life insurance. (*quick beat*) Where the hell've you been tonight? The one night I wanna see you, the one time I look forward to hanging around this armpit of an apartment with you, and you're not here! (*MARTHA is laughing again, silently this time, hands covering her face. After a moment, she stops.*)

MARTHA. Oh, boy. (*looks at JACK*) Guess what happened. My dad came to see me at work. (*laughs*) It was real comical. Guess what he did. He hired private eyes to find me. Then he came up from Florida, with his new wife. Guess how surprised he was to see he's a grandpa. He's got this young wife and now he's a grandpa. He about bust a gasket. Pounding on the desk and . . . yelling things at me. He . . . tried to slap me. Everybody's staring. He tole me I'm sick! Sick! (*Beat: she struggles to calm herself.*) So I took the day off. (*laughs*) I ran away. I just . . . I dunno what I did, I walked. Then I called him. He always stays at the Hyatt. If there's no Hyatt, he doesn't go. (*pauses*) Grow up, he says. See a shrink. Get treatment. Go back to school, don't dress so funny. He thinks I'm just a cute little time bomb. I'm not crazy! (*looks at JACK*) You think I am?

JACK. Marty, I . . .

MARTHA. You said so a coupla times. I feel like the only sane person in the world.

JACK. Well, certainly in this room.

MARTHA. My dad says feeling like that's a sure sign

you're insane. (*The TELEPHONE rings, once.*) I'm not talking to him!

JACK'S ANSWERING MACHINE VOICE. Hi! If you wanna leave a message for Jack — (*JACK stands, goes to the machine.*) — or Martha, please wait till you hear the . . . (*JACK turns the volume off.*)

MARTHA. (*holding her stomach, rocking back and forth, and talking to her child*) Sh. Sh. Go back to sleep. It's okay. (*smiles at Jack*) She slept through the whole thing. (*beat*) You think I'm crazy?

JACK. I used to think so, yeah. It's why I was crazy about you.

MARTHA. (*laughs*) Ooh. Sometimes I think she uses my bladder for a punching bag, I have to pee about every three minutes. (*to her belly*) Stop it.

JACK. Sit down, babe. What would your dad say if he saw you talking to your belly?

MARTHA. (*sits*) That I'm nuts. Hey, know what one of the women at class said? That they can recognize voices.

JACK. Fetuses? Fetoi? Really?

MARTHA. So when they're born, they know who their fathers are, 'cause they can recognize their voice.

JACK. That's not true!

MARTHA. Oh, sure.

JACK. So, some day, years from now, if there's anything left to sit on, she'll be watching the late show, and she'll leap to her feet — (*leaps to his feet*) — and say, "Dad! I'd recognize that golden voice anywhere!" (*Beat. Then he gets down on his hands and knees, talks to MARTHA's stomach.*) Jack here. Your . . . father. (*to MARTHA*) Technical terms are weird. (*back to the belly, in a smooth, silky actor voice*) The first piece I'm going to do for you tonight is from *A Midsummer Night's Dream.*

MARTHA. Oh!

JACK. (*recitative*) Oh, grim-looked night. Oh, night with hue so black.

MARTHA. I love this speech.

JACK. Oh, night, which ever art, when day is not. Oh, night. Oh, night! Alack, alack, alack. (*beat*) Oh, God. No wonder Stuart got the part. (*back to the belly*) Hey, kid, I got bad news. The world needs work. It's been overrun by tourists and there's a good chance civilization'll self-destruct in the next few years. But don't blame me. None a this is my fault.

MARTHA. Jack.

JACK. But there's beer. And wine, and movies, and music, and the Chicago Cubs. (*HE stops: a beat. Then JACK gently buries his head in MARTHA's lap.*)

MARTHA. (*strokes his hair, then lifts his head*) You crying?

JACK. Am I?

MARTHA. (*gently touches his eyes with her tongue*) Tastes like tears.

JACK. I'm a very good actor.

(*Tableau: MARTHA holds JACK, his head resting on her swollen stomach. LIGHTS fade slowly to BLACKOUT. And FADE UP: JACK alone, sitting on a bench, waiting, reading a script, glancing up from time to time, looking rather nervous. HE sees MARTHA off-stage, hides the script in his shoulder bag, stands, waves.*)

JACK. Marty! Over here!

MARTHA. (*enters*) What're you doing here?

JACK. Waiting for you.

MARTHA. Why didn't you come up to the office?

JACK. Oh, they're sick of me up there.

MARTHA. No, they like you a lot.

JACK. Really? (*MARTHA sits on the bench, tiredly.*) Bad day again?

MARTHA. Pretty bad. I got that heartburn again. I'm really beat.

JACK. (*a beat, then impulsively stands*) Let's eat. I'm craving a stuffed broccoli and fresh mushroom pizza.

MARTHA. Oh God.

JACK. Sounds good, eh?

MARTHA. I got class tonight.

JACK. To heck with class, let's do dinner.

MARTHA. I can't.

JACK. Your dad called.

MARTHA. (*slight pause*) Oh?

JACK. He said, "Jack? Martha's father here." I told him he had a real sexy voice. Not really. He would like you to call him. Collect. (*beat*) Ask him for some money.

MARTHA. No.

JACK. Why not.

MARTHA. That's just what he wants.

JACK. What's wrong with giving people what they want?

MARTHA. Because I can't.

JACK. I think you're being selfish. (*HE looks at her; no response.*) Damn it. Marty.

MARTHA. What?

JACK. I gotta catch a plane tonight. (*MARTHA looks at him.*) L.A.

MARTHA. Los Angeles? You're going to Los Angeles tonight?

JACK. Pretty weird, eh?

MARTHA. You're gonna be in a movie.

JACK. Test for a movie. Audition. (*laughs*) This is too weird. It's those same producers who did *The Chicago*

Story, they saw me in *Little Criminals*. They called Anita and I interviewed with the casting director today and the two of us are flying out to the coast tonight to read for the director. Apparently, the L.A. actor walked, and they're in a big hurry. It's a cop film, for TV. A real piece a shit, but a good part for me. Big part. (*takes out the script*) Well, I can't do it. Right now, I got the concentration of a spastic grasshopper.

MARTHA. Oh, Jack.

JACK. Interesting times.

MARTHA. When will you be back?

JACK. Tomorrow night. Probably.

MARTHA. What do mean, probably?

JACK. If I get the part, which I won't, but if I do, I'll be out there from five to ten weeks, depending on . . . how long I'll be out there. Postproduction and all that. Three, two, one, blastoff. (*pauses*) Marty. I'd be out there for . . . I mean, if I get the part, which I —

MARTHA. You will.

JACK. I'd miss the . . . grand entrance. I'd be out there when . . . (*an outburst*) God damn it! If this isn't the shittiest business in the world! Well, I won't get the part. I can't do it. I haven't got the chops to do work like this. I mean, who am I? The schmuck from Chicago, they'll laugh me right off the . . . sound stage.

MARTHA. You're gonna get the part.

JACK. I won't! Look at this beerbelly.

MARTHA. You'll get it.

JACK. Will you stop with the witch shit!

MARTHA. You must be really happy.

JACK. Happy!

MARTHA. You've been waiting for this to happen all your life. This is really great for you.

JACK. Don't make fun of me.

MARTHA. (*surprised*) I'm not.

JACK. Marty. What'll you do, if I . . . get the part?

MARTHA. Be happy for you.

JACK. No, I mean, what'll you . . . do? Will you be . . . ?

MARTHA. I'll be okay!

JACK. But will you need . . . ? (*quick beat*) Money, moral support, will you be able to get by without my charismatic presence in your life, bringing sunshine and joy to your otherwise drab existence? I don't wanna go!

MARTHA. You gotta go.

JACK. I'll call Anita and tell her I can't do it.

MARTHA. Don't be silly.

JACK. I don't wanna leave you! (*beat*) Well, I won't get the part!

MARTHA. (*shouts*) If you don't get this part, I'll never speak to you again! (*laughs*) You're gonna be on TV! (*beat*) I'll . . . see you on TV — I'll miss you. (*laughs nervously, with an edge of panic*) We never went to a ballgame. Jack. Jack! Oh!

JACK. What. Marty. What is it!?

MARTHA. (*after a pause, hands on her chest*) Heartburn.

JACK. Are you . . . ?

MARTHA. I'm fine. I got birthing class tonight. Tonight we're doing flutter breathing. That's because at the end of labor, sometimes, you get this tremendous urge to push, but you can't if the cervix isn't dilated enough, you could hurt the baby, or you could tear and rip the cervix. So you do the flutter breathing and it takes away the urge. (*beat*) This is exciting, Jack.

JACK. I feel like I should . . . stay here.

MARTHA. No. You gotta go.

JACK. Come to the airport with me.

MARTHA. I got class.
JACK. Marty.
MARTHA. Bye, Jack. (*stands, awkwardly, goes to Jack, hugs him*) Getting hard to hug.
JACK. Wish me bad luck.
MARTHA. I wish you all the luck in the world but you won't need it 'cause you're gonna be wonderful, I know you will.
JACK. Marty.
MARTHA. Break a leg.

(*A moment. Then MARTHA turns, rather abruptly, and exits. JACK picks up his shoulder bag and exits, opposite. LIGHTS fade to BLACKOUT. SFX, in the darkness: a JET PLANE taking off, roaring, climbing, then fading slowly away, to silence. LIGHTS fade slowly up: JACK's apartment, in the morning. MARTHA's overstuffed backpack lies in the middle of the room, along with some extra clothes. A moment: empty stage. Then NOISES off: a key in the lock. JACK enters, with his shoulder bag, as before, but now looking rumpled and haggard, very tired. HE sees MARTHA's pack, and stops short, staring at it.*)

MARTHA. (*offstage, in the bedroom*) Who is it? Who's there! Hey! Who's there!?! (*JACK closes the door.*) Who is it!!!
JACK. (*tiredly*) Me. Mr. L.A.
MARTHA. (*appears in the bedroom door*) Oh, God, Jack, you scared me. (*A moment. MARTHA calms herself. And JACK looks at her: SHE's wearing a new maternity dress, looking very nice.*) What are you doing here?
JACK. I came in on the redeye.

MARTHA. Didn't you get the part? You turned it down?

JACK. No. Yes. Don't panic. I got the part. I'm a superstar. You should see the hotel room they put me in. "Starlets in the lobby that'll make a man drool. Blood on the curtains, and a phone by the pool." I fly back tonight. Shooting starts tomorrow. How come you're not at work?

MARTHA. At work? Oh.

JACK. Nice dress.

MARTHA. Thanks.

JACK. How much was it?

MARTHA. Fifty-two dollars.

JACK. What's the occasion? (*quick beat*) Don't tell me, I got a feeling I don't wanna know. You wouldn't believe L.A., babe, it's the only city in the world with rabies. I think I should sit down. I'm very tired. I haven't slept in three days. No el in Los Angeles. I got a new agent. You'd hate her. She wears as much money as I make in two years. (*sits, slowly*) Going camping?

MARTHA. I'm going to Sylvia's.

JACK. Oh. (*short pause*) Why?

MARTHA. 'Cause I . . . need a friend right now. I called her. She thought I was mad at her, 'cause a the canoe trip, I guess I said some stuff, I don't remember. I was pretty crazy up in those woods. She and her lover just split up, so she needs a friend, too, and I'm —

JACK. Oh? Interesting. She needs a new friend, and you're — (*JACK stops himself.*) Shit. I'm sorry. I'm . . . sorry.

MARTHA. I gotta go in a minute.

JACK. No.

MARTHA. Yes.

JACK. Wanna go to Ann Sathers? Or some place

fancy? I've always wanted to have a hundred dollar breakfast. Dom Perignon.
MARTHA. I can't.
JACK. Please.
MARTHA. No.
JACK. Pretty please.
MARTHA. I can't.

(*JACK suddenly stands. MARTHA reacts, startled. Tense beat.*)

JACK. There any beer? (*Exits into the kitchen. MARTHA takes a deep breath, trying to relax. From offstage:*) Guess how much money I'm making. Double scale. That's five thousand two hundred a week. Plus they pay my agent's commission, plus two hundred a day per diem for the location stuff. Boy! I must really be good! (*appears in the kitchen door*) Wanna come out to L.A.? You'd like it there. Lots of artsy types.
MARTHA. That why you came back?
JACK. (*after a beat*) Lookit this. (*goes to his shoulder bag, takes out several books*) These books amaze me. They're all written in this folksy, gosh-having-babies-sure-brings-people-together style, and everytime I read 'em, I cry. (*MARTHA looks away. JACK reads.*) "My wife nudges me awake at three A.M. 'It's starting,' she whispers." And I've got tears rolling down my—
MARTHA. (*shouts*) Jack!!! What are you doing!?! Flying around the country on airplanes, reading birthing books?
JACK. Yeah.
MARTHA. You buy 'em at the airport?
JACK. Um . . . yeah. One of 'em. I got the other two at—

MARTHA. What are you doing!?!

JACK. (*stands, angrily*) That's me growing in your belly there! Me!!! (*Pause. JACK sits.*)

MARTHA. You want me to come out and have my baby in Hollywood?

JACK. Um . . . yeah. That's what I want. I can afford it.

MARTHA. What would I do, Jack? Sit at the Hyatt, waiting for labor to start?

JACK. Um . . . yeah. They got cable out there.

MARTHA. I called my dad.

JACK. You been busy.

MARTHA. Yeah.

JACK. He tell you how crazy you were? How sick you were? Did he politely suggest the best thing would be for you to jump under the Clark Street bus?

MARTHA. I did most a the yelling. He's gonna send me some money. And he wants to come up for the . . .

JACK. The grand entrance.

MARTHA. I said . . . okay. He said he's . . . (*laughs*) . . . excited, to be a . . . (*stops*) Jack. (*Beat: MARTHA takes a deep, calming breath; SHE's pretty shaky.*) I'm very proud of this. There's so many people who want children and can't have them, and so many people who can, and they kill them. (*smiles*) Look what they did.

JACK. We're very talented.

MARTHA. (*suddenly passionate*) The world's not gonna blow up, Jack! Your talent's not gonna go away! I'm not crazy! And she's gonna be alright, that's the only important thing. The only important thing.

JACK. So where you going all dressed up?

MARTHA. Sylvia's.

JACK. Yeah?

MARTHA. Then to Oak Park.

JACK. What's in . . . ? (*quick beat*) I got it all figured out, the way it works. Jack the genius. It's knowing you're okay, that it makes perfect sense that there should be smaller versions of yourself, walking around loose, it's the most natural thing in the world. In fact, the world'll be better off with a Jack and Martha junior in it. Creative egotism. This all came to me, in a flash, somewhere over Provo, Utah. And it's gonna be a boy! (*pauses*) What's in Oak Park?

MARTHA. Adoption agency. (*JACK again stands abruptly and MARTHA reacts, frightened.*) Jack! You scare me when you do that.

JACK. So how's it work? You sign on the dotted line and they yank him out from between your legs, then carry him screaming through the double doors? Hand him to some stranger from the suburbs? "'Bye. Have a nice one. Vote Democratic and thanks for the memories," just like that? Easy.

MARTHA. Easy. You think it's gonna be easy? It'll be the hardest thing I'll ever do.

JACK. Then why are you doing it!

MARTHA. Because this is not a world that's very kind to twenty-year-old dancers with a baby, and no money, and no place to live. I'm not ready to be a mother, Jack, if you thought about it, you'd see that.

JACK. She's the only real thing I've ever done!

MARTHA. She's not a thing! (*short pause*) She's not a thing.

JACK. (*Pause. Sits on the sofa.*) Well. I guess it's the logical thing. Who are we, anyway? Actors, shit. It's all we can do to feed ourselves, much less some kid. Coupla crazy, kooky kids like us. Actors! (*quick beat*) Hey, there ya go. I bet they'll pay a real premium for our kid. A couple young, intelligent artistes like us. Pretty. Healthy. White. That's important, isn't it? White people like us, most white people abort their mistakes, right? A pair of totally functional, top of the line adults like us, they'll pay top dollar. Whatever you do, for Christ sake, don't tell 'em I'm Irish Catholic, they'll knock twenty-five percent right off the top! (*stands*) You thief! Fucking sperm thief! The money and the time you've stolen from me, I've wasted nine months on you, you shit, you crazy little shit! And now you're gonna take it away from me, god damn it, and what'm I gonna do? My work is shit, Los Angeles is shit, I'm nothing but shit! Marty! Marty! (*beat*) Please don't walk away from me. Everything I want's there in your belly. I don't have anything else. If you take it away, I'll die. I'll die. (*pauses*) I'll die. (*laughs*) Hey, look at me. Giving the performance of a lifetime. Too bad the Jeff Committee isn't here. I'm gonna be a star. A dream come true. I don't think I'll ever sleep again. (*beat*) I'm gonna die. (*JACK looks at MARTHA, then looks away.*) You better go to Sylvia's. Go on. I'll be okay. Go on. Go on! (*MARTHA stands, slowly shoulders her pack, and starts to exit.*) Okay.

MARTHA. (*stops, turns*) What?

JACK. Okay. (*MARTHA exits.*) Okay. (*A moment. Then JACK stands, and comes downstage. LIGHTS roll: JACK is isolated, no longer in the apartment. SFX: a JET taking off, as before, roaring and climbing, then fading.*) Los Angeles was fogged in that evening, so the plane landed in Las Vegas, where I spent seventy-five dollars playing slot machines in the airport, till the plane finally left, arriving in L.A. at one A.M., five hours before shooting began. The black starless sky, the black sea, the city glowing like a decomposing corpse. (*pauses*) It was hard work. Very boring, after all the stage work I'd done, and the food was terrible. The director was one of those artist types. A real prick. I refused to fight with the writers, like most of the actors, I guessed more or less to pass the time. I knew no amount of rewriting would make the picture any better, so I let it go. The writers all thought I was a wimp, but the director loved me. (*pauses*) I thought about Marty, more or less constantly, but I didn't try to call her. One day, one of the assistant producers gave me a letter, a certified letter from a law firm in Chicago, representing an adoption agency in Oak Park. Who represented Marty. It contained a . . . release for me to sign, as the father of Marty's child. I signed it. I . . . (*Long pause: JACK looks at the floor, then looks up, composed.*) It went well. Everyone assured me my future was as bright as L.A. itself. I made a lot of new friends. Shallow people lead active social lives. They can't see the corpses. (*MARTHA enters. SHE's wearing jeans and a sweater — no longer pregnant. SHE stands very still, separated from JACK by shadow, not looking at him.*) I never saw Marty again. I came back to Chicago, and no one asked me about her. What could I have said? Everybody treated me like a leper. The el kept me awake all night. (*SFX: the electronic BEEP of JACK's answering machine.*)

MARTHA. Jack? Martha. I'm in Florida. I'm gonna go study dance again, in Connecticut. You're in Los Angeles maybe. My dad's giving me a whole year free tuition at . . . this college in Connecticut. I lost your address, but that's okay. (*pauses*) I'm . . . okay. Labor was very hard, it lasted for thirty hours. My dad was there, and Sylvia. They had to give me a lot of drugs, so I'm still a little — (*SFX: an electronic BEEP, cutting her off. Pause, then SFX: another BEEP.*) Well, it's a boy, you fucker. I think he's gonna have brown eyes like yours and he didn't have any hair at all. He was great. Is great. There's at least three very happy people in the world, because of what we did. (*beat*) It was . . . I mean, after all the—Well, it was even harder than I—(*beat*) I'm gonna call you back in a minute, okay? (*Pause. SFX: the answering machine BEEP.*) My dad's gonna freak when he sees his phone bill. But I wanna say . . . I miss you. And that I've learned a lot from you, you've been a real teacher to me. I'd like it if I could see you again, but I don't know when that could be. (*pauses*) So . . . 'Bye, Jack. 'Bye. I love you. (*A moment. MARTHA slowly exits.*)

JACK. (*alone*) Good-bye.

(*Tableau. LIGHTS fade slowly to BLACKOUT.*)

CURTAIN

PROPERTY PLOT

ACT I ONSTAGE
Radiator
Baseball bat and glove
Telephone bench
Answering machine
Phone books
Bookshelves
Cans
Playboy magazine
Movie goer magazine
2 *Sports Illustrated* magazines
The *Chicago Sun Times*
Manilla folders
Table and 2 chairs
Reviews on door
Stack of *The New York Times*
2 floor pillows
Phone
Records
Radio
Postcards and reviews
Trunk
Rolling Stone Magazine
Life magazine
Reader magazine
Postcards on post
Sofa with sofa pillows
Rug
Bills

UPSTAGE LEFT
LITTLE CRIMINALS
Father books

$52.00 in *LITTLE CRIMINAL* pants
Jack's shoulder bag
LA script

UPSTAGE RIGHT
Bag with a six pack of beer
Glass of soda water
Paper in a pack
Tackle box
Martha's back pack
Spray bottle

UPSTAGE CENTER
2 glasses of water
Guest check pad
Restaurant tent card
1 pitcher of milk
6 German beers
Afghan blanket
2 sets of silver in napkins
Pen
2 glasses of milk
1 Guiness Stout beer
Dish towel

(For the Characters)

ACT I JACK
Checkbook in tan jacket
Wristwatch
Wallet with over $200.00 inside

ACT I MARTHA
Watch
Purse

Cloth napkin

ACT TWO ONSTAGE
1 plant on table
Directory of adoptions on table
1 plant on top of bookshelves
Water jar on table
1 plant in front of phone
New magazines and papers on trunk

UPSTAGE RIGHT
Industrial script
Jack's bills

UPSTAGE LEFT
Magazine
Clock
Wire whisk
Beer
The Mother Earth News
Film Comment magazine
Planned parenthood material
Ice tray
Fan with extension cord
The New Yorker
Vanity Fair

COSTUME PLOT

ACT I JACK

SCENE 1
Pants
Brown loafers
Brown plaid shirt
Suede jacket

SCENE 5
Tennis shoes
White shirt
Corduroy jacket

SCENE 7
Suit
Black loafers
Tie

SCENE 8
Tan corduroy trousers
Brown loafers
Tweed jacket

ACT II JACK

SCENE 1
Brown loafers
White shirt
Corduroy trousers
Clip on tie
Tweed jacket

SCENE 2
Green T-shirt

SCENE 3
Running shorts

SCENE 4
Corduroy trousers
Plaid shirt
Black socks
Brown shoes
Suede jacket
Watch

ACT I MARTHA

SCENE 1
Turquoise sweater
Jeans
Tennis shoes
White socks
Apron

SCENE 2
Army jacket
Purse
(Remove apron)

SCENE 3
Add apron

SCENE 5
Army jacket
Backpack

SCENE 8
Pregnant pad
India shirt
Old tennis shoes

ACT II MARTHA

SCENE 1
Tennis shoes
Brown pants
Plaid shirt

SCENE 2
Sleeveless dress
Low heel shoes
Purse

SCENE 4
Bigger pregnant pad
India shirt
Brown pants
Tennis shoes

SCENE 5
Purse
Blue maternity dress
Low heel shoes

SCENE 6
Jeans
Turquoise sweater
Low heel shoes

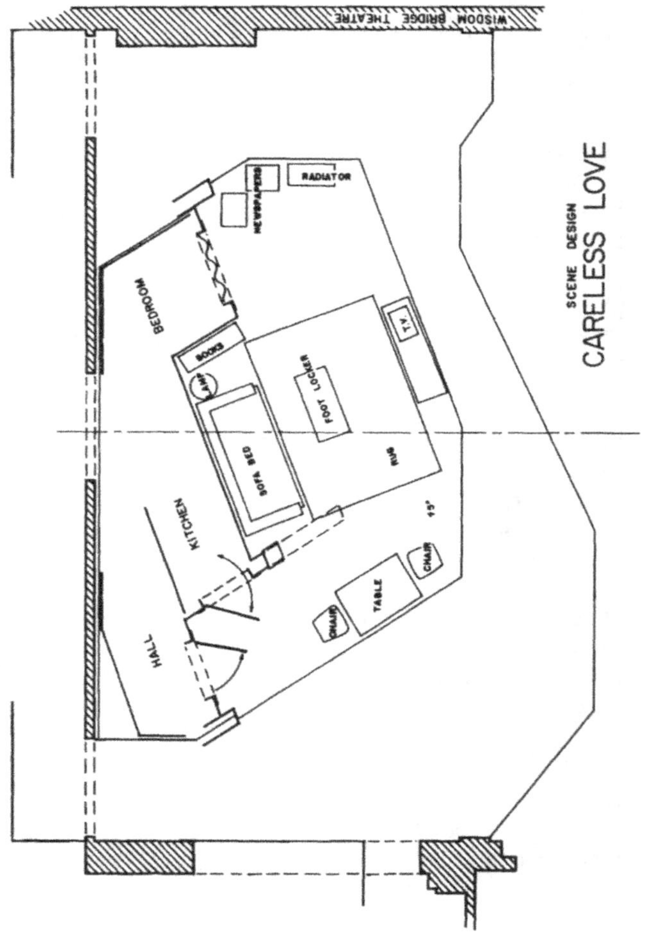

WISDOM BRIDGE THEATRE
SCENE DESIGN
CARELESS LOVE
BEDROOM
NEWSPAPERS
RADIATOR
SOCKS
LAMP
SOFA BED
FOOT LOCKER
T.V.
RUG
KITCHEN
HALL
CHAIR
TABLE
CHAIR
15°